PECOS BILL and the MUSTANG

PECOS BILL and the MUSTANG

by
Harold W. Felton

Pictures by
LEONARD SHORTALL

PRENTICE-HALL, INC., ENGLEWOOD CLIFFS, N. J.

OTHER P-H BOOKS BY HAROLD W. FELTON:
BOWLEG BILL: *Seagoing Cowpuncher*
NEW TALL TALES OF PECOS BILL

Pecos Bill and the Mustang, by Harold W. Felton
© 1965 by Prentice-Hall, Inc., Englewood Cliffs, New Jersey
All rights reserved, including the right to reproduce this
book or any portions thereof, in any form, except for the in-
clusion of brief quotations in a review.

Printed in the United States of America

Library of Congress Catalog Card number: 65-17809
T-65558

PRENTICE-HALL INTERNATIONAL, INC., *London*
PRENTICE-HALL OF AUSTRALIA, PTY., LTD., *Sydney*
PRENTICE-HALL OF CANADA, LTD., *Toronto*
PRENTICE-HALL OF INDIA (PRIVATE) LTD., *New Delhi*
PRENTICE-HALL OF JAPAN, INC., *Tokyo*

U.S. 1327873

Did you ever hear of Pecos Bill?

He was a cowboy. The first cowboy. He invented cowboys and everything about them and he became the hero of all the other rootin' tootin', high falootin', straight shootin' cowboys.

He could shoot a bumblebee in the eye at sixty paces, and he was a man who was not afraid to shake hands with lightning.

But before he became a man, he was a boy, and before he was a boy, he was a baby.

That seems only reasonable, doesn't it?

Bill was born a long time ago, away out in the wild and woolly west.
It was so long ago the sun was only about the size of a dime. Of
course, money went farther in those days, so naturally a dime was bigger
than it is now.

Bill always obeyed his parents. They used to say he was the best
child they ever saw and that was quite a compliment because he had
seventeen brothers and sisters.

One day, Bill's family saw smoke from a new neighbor's chimney.
It was beyond the river and two hills but Bill's paw allowed the
country was getting too crowded. Bill's maw agreed. They liked plenty
of elbow room, so they decided to move farther west.

So they loaded their wagon with all their household goods and their
eighteen children, and off they went over the Texas plains, across the
rivers, and over the mountains and the valleys.

They came to the Pecos River and crossed it. Then the left hind wheel hit a prairie dog hole. The wagon lurched, and Bill fell out.

He landed head first on a rock. The rock broke into a thousand pieces, and Bill's head was bruised, a little.

The wagon juggled and rumbled away into the distance, toward the setting sun.

When Bill came to he didn't know where he was or who he was. He didn't know what to do or how to do it.

He didn't remember a single thing about his life, his maw and paw, or his seventeen brothers and sisters.

He was all alone on the west bank of the Pecos River in West Texas.

He didn't know his age, either, so no one knows exactly how old he was. But he was a little shaver, only about half as high as the withers of a pinto pony.

An old coyote rescued him. The coyote's name was *El Viejo,* which means *Old Man* in Spanish.

El Viejo didn't know what the little boy's name was or what to call him. Finally, he called him Pecos Bill, and took him to live with the coyotes.

So Pecos Bill grew up with the coyotes. He learned to walk like

a coyote. He learned to talk like a coyote. He thought he *was* a coyote.

That was only natural considering that he had lost his memory when he

fell out of the wagon and broke the rock into a thousand pieces and

bruised his head, a little.

His playmates were coyote pups. He wrestled with them and they

yipped and yapped and growled playfully at him and nipped each other.

Bill learned to howl at the moon. He learned to scratch his ear with his foot, and he could run fast enough to catch a rabbit.

When he got older he could run down an antelope without losing his breath.

Then, one day, Pecos Bill met a *man*. The man said, "Who are you?"

"I'm a coyote pup," Bill growled.

"You don't look like a coyote to me," said the man. "You look like a human."

"I am not a human," Bill snarled. "I'm a coyote and that's all there is to it!"

"If you're a coyote, where is your tail?" the man asked with a grin.

Bill looked over his shoulder. He couldn't see a tail. He must have a tail. All the coyotes Bill knew had long, bushy tails.

He must have a tail. He must. After all, he was a coyote, wasn't he? At least he thought he was.

Bill looked around again, this time under his arm. He couldn't see a tail. Not even a little one.

There must be some mistake!

He backed up to a stream and looked at his reflection in the water.

It was true! He didn't have a tail! No tail at all!

If he didn't have a tail he couldn't be a coyote.

If he wasn't a coyote, he must be a human.

And that is how Pecos Bill discovered he was a human and not a coyote.

Then he decided that if he wasn't a coyote he shouldn't be living with coyotes.

So he barked "goodbye" to *El Viejo* and he yipped "so long pals" to

his coyote pup friends and started off with the man.

"As long as I'm a human, I'm going to be a cowboy," he said.

"And if I'm going to be a *cowboy,* I'll need a horse."

"What's a cowboy?" the man asked.

"That's easy. He's a man who rounds up cattle," Bill answered.

"You won't need a horse," the man said. "We only have tame cows

and you don't need a horse for tame cows."

"There are wild longhorn cattle around these parts," said Bill.
"There are wild horses and other wild critters. No sir! I'll need a
horse because I aim to round up and catch those wild longhorns!"

But Pecos Bill was too big for an ordinary horse.

The biggest animal in that part of the country was a mountain lion.
A long haired, long tailed, long toothed mountain lion.

Bill captured the mountain lion and broke him to ride.

The mountain lion didn't like it much, at first. He was quite peevish
about it. He was as peevish as a bee with a boil.

But he soon learned to like Pecos Bill and became quite friendly.

He liked to have Pecos scratch him behind the ears. That made him purr. When Bill's mountain lion purred, he sounded like a freight train rumbling by.

By this time, Bill was almost full grown, and he was big. No one knows exactly *how* big, but he was big enough to chase bears with a switch.

Bill slept on a gravel bed, between sandpaper sheets. He used a soft rock for a pillow. On cold nights, he pulled a blanket of fog over him.

He shaved with his bowie knife. Not with the knife itself—it was too sharp. He used its shadow to shave as it was quite sharp enough.

One day, a rattlesnake bit him. It was a tough, mean rattlesnake and challenged Bill to a fight.

Pecos Bill was a gentle man. He didn't like to fight, but the rattler insisted.

Bill won that fight, too, and he used the rattlesnake for a *quirt* or
riding whip. The rattler liked the job. It was something not every
rattlesnake got a chance to do.

It was quite a sight to see Pecos Bill riding his mountain lion on a dead run, kicking up a cloud of dust and sandburrs and using the rattler for a quirt.

But Pecos Bill wanted a horse. To be exact, he wanted the Famous Pacing Mustang of the Prairies.

No one had ever been able to catch the mustang and ride him. They said even bullets could not stop him. Few men had ever even seen him.

Pecos Bill thought the Famous Pacing Mustang of the Prairies was the horse for him.

He rode far out on the prairie until he found the herd of wild horses led by the great Pacing Mustang.

He gasped when he saw the horse. He was a palomino. His shining coat was the color of a new minted gold coin. His mane and tail were snowy white. He had four white stockings and a white blaze between the eyes, and Bill made up his mind to capture him that very day.

Bill mounted his mountain lion. He lifted his quirt and his
rattlesnake rattled.

The mountain lion roared and dug his claws in the ground. Cactus
and tumbleweed swirled up in the dusty air as he shot forward like
a bullet.

The Famous Pacing Mustang of the Prairies saw them coming and began to run away. But it was too late. Bill's galloping mountain lion rushed toward the mustang. They were running side by side.

In another instant, the mustang would draw ahead. There was no time to lose. Bill had to act! At once!

The mountain lion roared. The rattlesnake rattled. Pecos Bill

dropped his quirt and sprang from the mountain lion to the back of the

Famous Pacing Mustang of the Prairies!

No one had ever been astride the mustang before.

The mustang jumped and bucked and twisted and turned. But Pecos

Bill kept his seat.

"Yipee!" Bill yelled.

The mustang ran and kicked. Bill stayed on.

The mustang reared and pawed the air. Bill could not be thrown off.

The horse covered the land from the Platte River in Nebraska to the
Pecos River in Texas, from the Mississippi River to the Pacific Ocean.

There was pin wheeling, high diving, sun fishing, high flying and all
the other tricks of a bucking bronco.

But Bill stayed astride, waving his hat and shouting at the top of

his voice, "Yippee-ee-ee!"   U. S. 1327873

Pecos thought the mustang would never stop bucking, so he spoke

to him. He told the horse how he wanted to be a cowboy, how he

wanted to ride the range and lasso wild longhorn cattle and drive

them to market.

He told the mustang he needed a good horse to help him. If he
didn't have a horse that was good enough he might quit trying to be
a cowboy and go back to being a coyote again.

"I won't argue with you anymore," Pecos said. "I won't try to break
you anymore. If you don't want to help me, you go your way, and
I'll go mine."

Bill turned away and lay down to drink from the river.

The Famous Pacing Mustang of the Prairies came to his side.

He put his big nose in the water and he drank with Bill.

It was a sign that the mustang wanted to belong to Pecos Bill.

They both drank. They drank so much the river went down three inches.

Pecos Bill had a horse at last!

And that is how Pecos Bill got his first horse and became the first cowboy.